Noddy and the Treasure Map

HarperCollins *Children's Books*

It was a sunny day in Toyland and Noddy was looking for something exciting to do.

"Oh! Hello, Bumpy Dog," said Noddy. "I wish there was something exciting to do."

"Woof, woof!" suggested Bumpy Dog.

"An adventure?" cried Noddy.

"That's a great idea! Let's get some googleberry pie and think about it!"

At Miss Pink Cat's Ice Cream Parlour, the Goblins were trying to get googleberry treats for free.

"Don't you know it is 'Give Everything to Goblins for Free Day'?" Gobbo asked Miss Pink Cat.

"I won't give anything free to the two of you!" replied Miss Pink Cat.

Miss Pink Cat turned and saw Noddy. "Ah, a
paying customer!"

"Hello, Miss Pink Cat," Noddy called. "I'd like
to buy two slices of googleberry pie for Bumpy
Dog and me!"

"Did you say Bumpy Dog?" Miss Pink Cat
looked up in surprise. "He'd better not…"

"…jump on me again!"

But it was too late. Bumpy Dog had already knocked Miss Pink Cat over!

"I'm sorry," apologised Noddy. "Bumpy Dog is excited because we are planning an adventure."

Miss Pink Cat went to get Noddy's googleberry pie. "Both of you wait out here!" she ordered.

The naughty Goblins were still trying to think of a way to get some googleberry treats for free.

"Did you hear that, Sly?" asked Gobbo. "Noddy wants to go on an adventure. Quick, pass me a piece of paper and a crayon! I think I know how to get some money for googleberry treats!"

"Wow, Sly!" Gobbo said very loudly. "We will have quite an adventure with this treasure map!"

"But we just drew it…" Sly began to say until Gobbo nudged him. "Ow! I mean, yes, Gobbo, quite an adventure."

"Did you say adventure?" asked Noddy.

"Oh, hello, Noddy!" said Gobbo, pretending that he had not seen Noddy. "Yes, Sly and I were going to go on an adventure with this map but we have to… um…"

"…have tea with Mr Plod!" added Sly.

Gobbo grinned at Noddy. "I suppose we could sell it to you, Noddy. For two coins!"

Noddy looked at Bumpy Dog.

"Woof!" barked Bumpy Dog, eagerly.

"Done!" Noddy cheered, shaking Gobbo's hand.

"Just follow the map and you'll find the treasure inside that tree," said Gobbo. "Goodbye and good luck!"

Noddy was so excited to be going on an adventure that he sang a song:

A hat! A tie!
A cake! A pie!
Who knows what I'll find
On my treasure hunt!

Noddy and Bumpy Dog set off to follow the treasure map.

"The map says 'hop backwards five times down the street'." said Noddy. "Oh, well, if the map says so!" And Noddy began to hop backwards down the street.

"Ha, ha!" laughed Gobbo. "Now we can buy some googleberry treats with Noddy's money."

Next, the map told Noddy to 'Go inside the barn and tickle the cow.'

"Oh, well," thought Noddy. "If the treasure map says so, I had better follow the instructions."

But the cow didn't want to be tickled!

"Mooooo!" complained the cow.

Noddy and Bumpy Dog ran away.

A little while later Noddy and Bumpy Dog found themselves in the Dark Woods.

"It's kind of spooky in here," said Noddy.

"Woof!" agreed Bumpy Dog, standing very close to Noddy.

"But the treasure map says we need to come here. And if the treasure map says so, then we must."

"Woof!" Bumpy Dog was not so sure.

"It also says we need to sneeze twice and take seven steps to the left. Oh, well if the treasure map says so!" sneezed Noddy.

"Now what does the map say?" wondered Noddy.

"Call out Sly and Gobbo are fine fellows!" Noddy looked at Bumpy Dog.

"Oh, well if the map says so!"

"Sly and Gobbo are fine fellows!" shouted Noddy.

Big-Ears was picking mushrooms nearby. He came to see why Noddy was shouting.

"Hello, Noddy, Bumpy Dog," said Big-Ears. "What are you doing all the way out here?"

"We're on an adventure," said Noddy, excitedly. "We are going to find treasure!"

Big-Ears laughed. "You silly little Noddy. There's no treasure out here!"

"But the map says so!" cried Noddy. "We have followed all the instructions. The treasure is inside a big tree."

Noddy looked at the map one more time. He pointed to a nearby tree.

"And there it is! See?"

Big-Ears gasped.

   Noddy went to have a closer look at the tree.
"The treasure is inside that tree! But there is no
opening!"

   "Hmmm," said Big-Ears. "There is nothing in
this tree but wood."

"Where did you get this treasure map, Noddy?" asked Big-Ears.

"Sly and Gobbo sold it to me for two coins!" Big-Ears shook his head.

"Oh, no!" sighed Noddy, suddenly realising, "I've fallen for another Goblin trick!"

Big-Ears looked thoughtful. "I think it is about time we drew our own treasure map."

Back in Toy Town Square, Sly and Gobbo were
wondering how they were going to get more
money to buy *more* googleberry treats.

"Look, Gobbo!" shouted Sly. "It's Noddy and
he has lots of money with him."

Gobbo and Sly rushed over to Noddy.

"Wow, Noddy. Where did you get all that money?" asked Gobbo.

"It was all in the big tree," answered Noddy, "just like your treasure map said."

"It was?!" gasped Sly!

"And there was another treasure map in the tree, too!" replied Noddy.

"We sold you our treasure map, so, you should sell us yours!" insisted Gobbo.

The greedy Goblins would do anything to get their hands on some treasure.

But Noddy did not want to give in quite so easily.

"I don't know. I like finding treasure," he said.

"We'll give you four coins for it!" said Sly.

"Yeah, four coins," agreed Gobbo.

"Well…" said Noddy. "All right then."

"Quick, Sly! What's the first instruction on the map?" shouted Gobbo.

Noddy and Big-Ears were watching the Goblins following the map. But Noddy was not smiling.
"What's the matter, Noddy?" asked Big-Ears.
"I wanted to have an adventure today," sighed Noddy. "But I didn't even find real treasure. Only the mushrooms that we put in the fake money bag."

"But you did have an adventure!" said Big-Ears. "You gathered supplies, followed a map, travelled to many places, fooled some Goblins, and made some money. Sounds like an adventure to me!"

Noddy smiled. "Did you hear that Bumpy Dog?
We did have an adventure after all."
   Noddy was so happy he sang his song:
      It's fun
      To play
      To roam
      All day
      Adventuring is always a treasure hunt!

Meanwhile, Sly was still reading the map to Gobbo.
"Ok, Gobbo. Now you have to twirl around
until you get really dizzy and fall down," said Sly.
"Are you sure we should be doing this?"
wondered Gobbo.
"Yes! All we have to do is follow the map and
we'll be rich! Whoa-whoa-whoa…and dizzy!"

Noddy and Big-Ears laughed.

   "Silly Goblins," said Noddy. "I hope they have as much fun with their treasure map as I had with mine!"

   "Don't worry, Noddy," promised Big-Ears. "They will!" Noddy and Big-Ears laughed.

First published in Great Britain by HarperCollins Children's Books in 2005
HarperCollins Children's Books is a division of HarperCollins Publishers Ltd,
77-85 Fulham Palace Road, Hammersmith, London W6 8JB

1 3 5 7 9 10 8 6 4 2

Text and images copyright © 2005 Enid Blyton Ltd (a Chorion company).
The word "Noddy" is a registered trademark of Enid Blyton Ltd. All rights reserved.
For further information on Noddy and the Noddy Club please contact www.Noddy.com

ISBN 0-00-721056-6

A CIP catalogue for this title is available from the British Library.
The HarperCollins website address is:
www.harpercollinschildrensbooks.co.uk

Printed and bound by
Printing Express Ltd, Hong Kong

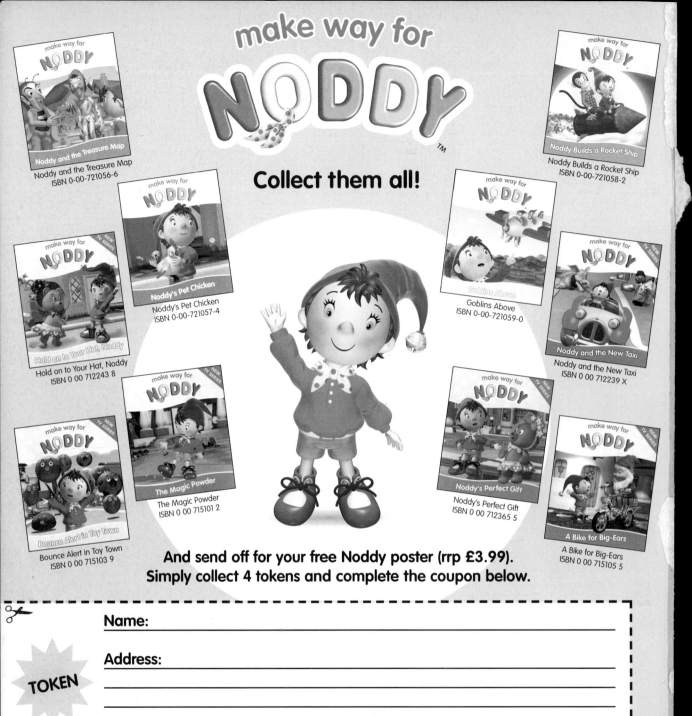

make way for NODDY ™

Collect them all!

Noddy and the Treasure Map
ISBN 0-00-721056-6

Noddy Builds a Rocket Ship
ISBN 0-00-721058-2

Noddy's Pet Chicken
ISBN 0-00-721057-4

Goblins Above
ISBN 0-00-721059-0

Hold on to Your Hat, Noddy
ISBN 0 00 712243 8

Noddy and the New Taxi
ISBN 0 00 712239 X

The Magic Powder
ISBN 0 00 715101 2

Noddy's Perfect Gift
ISBN 0 00 712365 5

Bounce Alert in Toy Town
ISBN 0 00 715103 9

A Bike for Big-Ears
ISBN 0 00 715105 5

**And send off for your free Noddy poster (rrp £3.99).
Simply collect 4 tokens and complete the coupon below.**

TOKEN

Name:

Address:

e-mail:

Make Way For Noddy videos now available at all good retailers.

UNIVERSAL